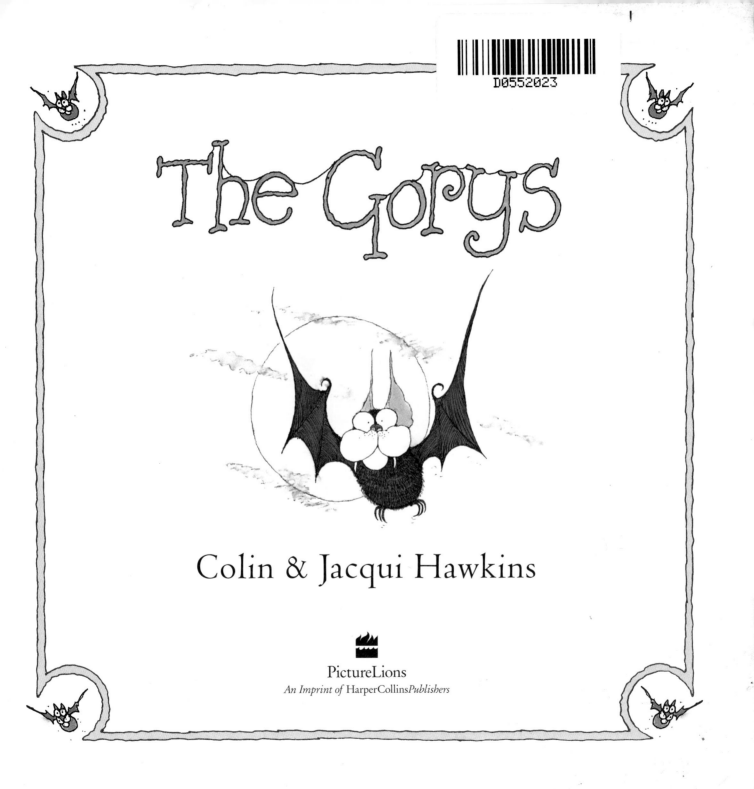

The Gorys

Colin & Jacqui Hawkins

PictureLions
An Imprint of HarperCollins*Publishers*

First published in Great Britain in Picture Lions by HarperCollins Publishers in 1999

I 3 5 7 9 10 8 6 4 2

ISBN: 0 00 664704 9
Picture Lions is an imprint of the Children's Division,
part of HarperCollins Publishers Ltd.
Text copyright © Colin and Jacqui Hawkins 1999
Illustrations copyright © Colin and Jacqui Hawkins 1999, 1982
The authors assert the moral right to be identified as the authors of the work.
A CIP catalogue record for this title is available from the British Library.
All rights reserved. No part of this publication may be reproduced, stored in a retrieval
system or transmitted in any form or by any means, electronic, mechanical,
photocopying, recording or otherwise, without the prior permission of HarperCollins
Publishers Ltd, 77-85 Fulham Palace Road, Hammersmith, London W6 8JB.
The HarperCollins website address is: www.fireandwater.com
Printed and bound in Singapore by Imago

The Gory Vampires

If you're feeling just a little bit wary,

And you think that all vampires are scary,

Step inside, meet the family Gory –

They're all dying to tell you their story.

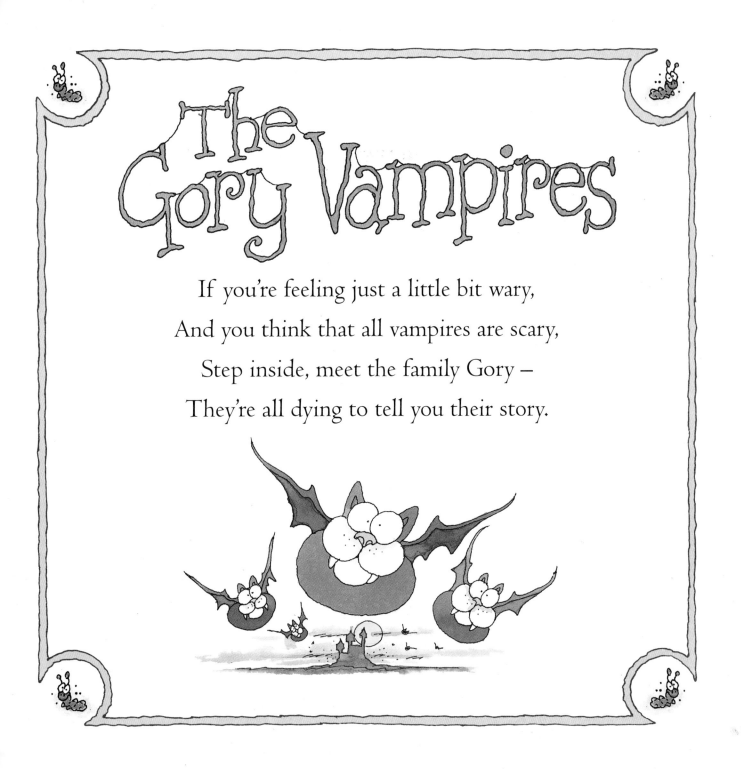

Gory Grange

The Gory family have lived at Gory Grange,
Cemetery Hill for hundreds and hundreds of
years. Over the centuries many a vampire horse
and carriage has rattled up the long, winding
drive and through the huge, iron gates up
to the ancient house.

Behind the great, oak front door, Gory Grange
is just like all vampire homes, with heavy, musty,
velvet curtains, huge stone fireplaces and
dark, gloomy furniture. Bats and spiders lurk
in every corner. Do come in and meet the family.

Meet the Gorys

Meet the Gorys, an ancient vampire family.
They are Mum and Dad, the twins
Val and Vlad, and baby Vasha.

"She's a little smasher," laughs Mum.
The Gory family pets are a dog called Fang,
a cat called Claw and, of course, being
vampires the family have lots and lots of
spiders and bats hanging around the house.

"We're all a bit batty in this
family," laughs Vlad the Dad.

Vlad the Dad

Varina

Vlad the Lad

Baby Vasha

Val

Fang

Claw

A Gory Day

Like all vampire families, the Gorys begin the day with breakfast. Val and Vlad have Dreaded Wheat cereal.

"It's fangtastic!" they giggle.

Baby Vasha has a bottle of Vibena juice and Dad reads his horrorscope in *The Daily Nightmare*.

On his way to work, Dad takes Val and Vlad to Cemetery Hill Junior School in the family hearse. They get there just as the bell clangs.

"Hurry up, Vlad. We'll be late for class," says Val. "It's Mr Howler's horrible history lesson."

"Ugh! Gruesome!" groans Vlad, and they both scurry into school.

Gory Work

After dropping the kids off at school Mr Gory arrives at his job. He is an undertaker and works for the *Fun Funerals and Barmy Burials* company.

"It's a grave business," says Mr Gory, "but we'll give you a funeral to die for!"

One of *Fun Funerals'* most popular burials is the 'Race to the Grave' service.

"We guarantee you'll go to the grave with a smile on your face," laughs Mr Gory proudly.

Granny Gory

Meanwhile, Mum and baby Vasha take
Fang the dog out for a walk through the graveyard.

"That's your great, great, great grandfather, Vlad
the Bad," says Mum to Vasha, pointing at a very
old tombstone.

Then they visit
Granny Gory
(Vlad the Dad's
mum), who lives

with lots of cats in a very old house. Granny loves
to play Incy Wincy Spider with baby Vasha.

A Gory Walk

Later, as the sun sets and shadows appear, the Gorys go for a walk in the park to feed the bats.

Val plays with her Varbie dolls and Vlad reads his favourite Batman comic to Fang.

Soon the sky is filled with the sounds of swirling, squeaking bats. EEK! EEK!

"This is my favourite time of the day," sighs Mum. "It's so creepy!"

The Gory family gather for supper.
Tonight, Val and Vlad have invited the kids
from next door to join them.

"Eat up dears, you've eaten necks
to nothing," chuckles Mum.

"But there's a spider in my soup!" wails one
of the visitors.

"Ooo! You lucky thing," shrieks Val.

"Mmm! That's hunky-gory!" says Dad, tucking into
his ghoulash. "I haven't had a bite all day!"

Bedtime Gory

The clock strikes twelve.

"Bedtime, kids," says Mum, "and don't forget to clean your fangs."

Val and Vlad creep up the dusty stairs to bed. Soon Mum comes up to read a bedtime story.

"I want a gory horror story," says Vlad.

"I want a scary fairy story," says Val.

Baby Vasha just gurgles at her bat-mobile.

Gory Story

"Are you sitting comfortably?" whispers Mum.

"Yes," giggles Val as she snuggles into bed.

"Once upon a time," says Mum, "there was a girl
called Little Red Riding Fang who lived in a dark wood…"

This is one of Val's favourite stories.

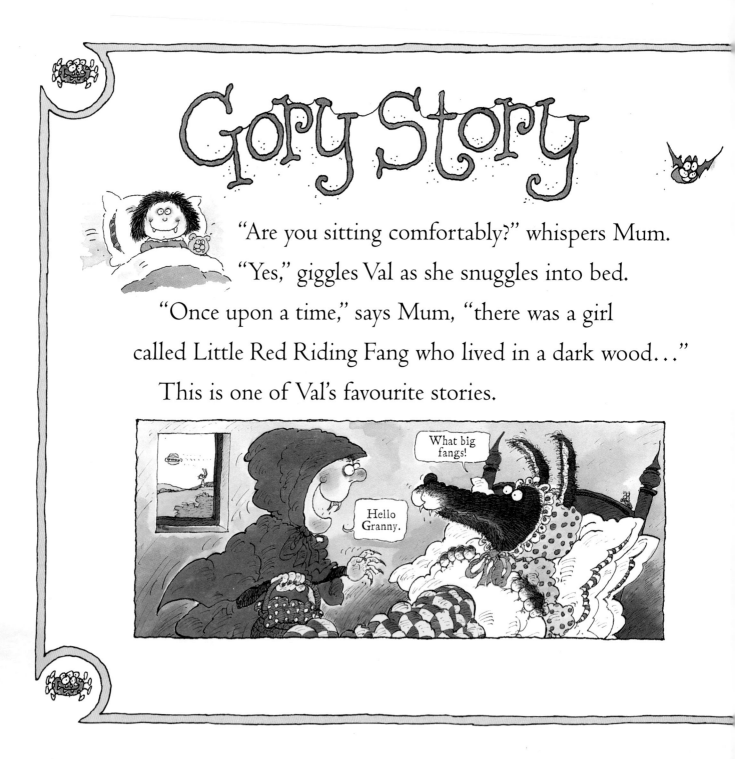

She also loves Vampirella and the Glass Fang – the story
of a poor but beautiful girl who married a prince.

But the story she loves most of all is Goldie Fang and
the Three Bears.

"I want gold fangs when I grow up!" says Val.

Gory Horror

"It's my turn for a story now," says Vlad. "I want a gory horror story."

Vlad loves terror tales, especially about his famous ancestors of long ago. So Mum tells Vlad all about Vlad the Bad, Vlad the Mad and Vlad the Sad. But his favourite vampire story is that of Great, Great, Great, Great Grandfather Vlad the Cad, who was a famous film star in the early days of Horrorwood.

"Goodnight kids. Sweet vampire dreams," whispers Mum, as she blows out the candles.

Gory Night

When the children are all asleep, Mum and Dad watch old vampire films on television.

"I love cousin Dracula. He's so funny," says Mum.

The clock chimes thirteen. Mum and Dad light a candle and go up the dark, spooky stairs to bed.

Good night. Sleep tight. Don't let the vampires bite.